D1575210

MONSTER HIGH ™

Drop Dead Diary

poppy

LITTLE, BROWN AND COMPANY
New York Boston

Poppy

Hachette Book Group
237 Park Avenue, New York, NY 10017
For more of your favorite series, visit our website at www.pickapoppy.com

Poppy is an imprint of Little, Brown and Company.
The Poppy name and logo are trademarks of Hachette Book Group, Inc.

First Edition: October 2011

ISBN 978-0-316-18661-2

10 9 8 7 6 5 4 3

SC

Printed in China

FRANKIE STEIN

MONSTER HIGH™

RAD Intel Party

NICKNAME: Firecracker

CATCHPHRASES: Mint! Voltage! Go green!

FAVORITE CLASS: History, to learn about her friends

LEAST FAVORITE CLASS: Phys ed—swimming causes short circuits!

PETS: Five lab rats called the Glitterati (and Dad's working on a dog)

MUST-CARRY ACCESSORY: Quilted handbag that doubles as a portable mini-charger

FAVE COLOR: Black-and-white stripes

BEDROOM SITCH: Turned her dad's lab into a Fab; sleeps in a totally RAD charging bed

BONUS TRIVIA
Can you name all of the Glitterati?

She's Got the Beat

Frankie loves to dance around the Fab. Program her playlist for your next dance party!

Ke$ha
"TiK ToK"

Alicia Keys
"No One"

Beyoncé
"Single Ladies
(Put a Ring on It)"

Lady Gaga
"The Fame"
"Just Dance"

Phoenix
"Lisztomania"

Basshunter
"Far From Home"

Wonder Girls
"Nobody"

Kings of Leon
"Use Somebody"

Willow Smith
"Whip My Hair"

Glee Cast
"I'll Stand By You"

Jackson Five
"I Want You Back"

BORN YESTERDAY

Frankie just came to life, so she's missed out on a lot of awesome TV, movies, and books. What would you put on her pop culture to-do list?

Must Read	Must-See TV	Must-See Movies

POWER PUZZLE

Know sudoku? This is like that, only CHARGEd up!

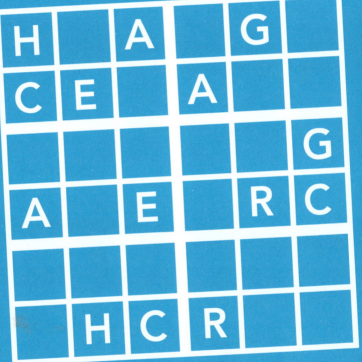

H		A		G	
C	E		A		
					G
A		E		R	C
	H	C	R		

CHARGE!

Monster Love

Frankie's new to the world and new to love! D.J., Billy, Brett . . . Chart her crushes on this graph.

Sparks fly with this flirtation.

_____

Can Frankie see him as more than a friend?

_____

He's Romeo to her Juliet.

_____

Stitched in Style

Frankie "seams" to have it all, but she wants a puppy too! Make your own Watzit felt puppy—or any other chic-freak friend!

You will need:

- Pieces of felt in freaky colors
- Thick yarn in contrasting colors
- A large tapestry or yarn needle
- Cotton batting or extra fabric for the stuffing
- Scissors
- Chalk
- *Optional: barrettes, safety pins, key chains, glue*

1 Sketch your design here. Then use chalk to draw your pattern on the felt.

2 Cut out the felt pieces and stitch them together. It doesn't have to be perfect—the freakier the better!

BONUS IDEA
Make tiny felt friends and glue them onto barrettes — or turn them into pins or key chains!

FREAK C'EST CHIC FASHION

Frankie loves mixing and matching patterns and styles. She'll pair combat boots with a plaid mini and then accessorize with beaded safety pins or a tie.

Look through your closet and plan some outfits for days when you feel like a fresh Frankie mix! Sketch the outfits on these pages for easy reference.

Change to Spare

Frankie hopes to change the world—she wants RADs and normies to live in harmony. What do you want to change in your world? Write about it on these pages.

Keep It Together!

GO GREEN!

MELODY CARVER

RAD Intel Party

NICKNAMES: Smellody, Melodork, Melly, Mel

CATCHPHRASE: *Can-dace!*

FAVORITE CLASS: Choir, now that her voice is back

LEAST FAVORITE CLASS: Computer science— she already knows how to send e-mails!

PETS: None…unless you count her sister, Candace

MUST-HAVE ACCESSORY: Iridescent feathers

FAVE COLOR: Black

BEDROOM SITCH: Lives in the former home of vampires, so the log-cabin vibe is dark, overheated, and sort of coffinlike

BONUS TRIVIA

What is the name of Melody's birth mom?

Meet and Greet

Melody just moved to Salem from the 90210. She needs to make some friends. What advice would you give her?

The World According to **Candace**

Mel's sister spouts advice like a leaky faucet. Here are a few of her choicest phrases.

You think about this stuff too much.

Curdy*boys are great practice.

PEOPLE STARE WHEN YOU'RE PRETTY.

Eyes on the prize, especially with guys.

Unpredictable is fun!

*curdy = cute + nerdy

It's diesel, you know. Good for the environment.

I SUGGEST A MAKEOVER. THEN A TAKEOVER. WHO'S WITH ME?

MY LASHES ARE VISIBLE FROM THE MOON BECAUSE OF MASCARA. REPEAT AFTER ME, MASS-CARE-*AHHH*.

Don't hate, tol-er-ate! It's un-NUDI to discriminate!

Come up with your own **Candace-ism** and write it here!

Candace Out!

Sketch Artist

Melody falls for Jackson right away when she sees him sketching at the carousel. Try your own hand at sketching. If you use pastels, as Jackson does, spray your finished drawing lightly with hair spray. That way, your masterpiece won't smudge!

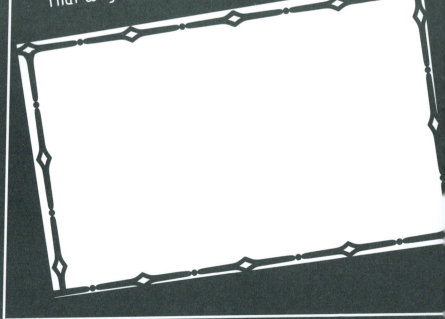

THE SIREN'S SONG

Melody used to sing all the time. What songs would you sing at an audition—or your next karaoke party?

FREAK C'EST CHIC FASHION

Melody likes to keep her look comfy and casual—but she still infuses style with bright-colored Chuck Taylors and vintage rock-band tees. Look through your closet and plan some casual outfits for days when you feel like a comfy, cute Melody look! Sketch the outfits on these pages for easy reference.

FREAK C'EST CHIC FASHION

Persuade Me

Melody learns the hard way that you can't just tell people what to do. Trying to make a case? Here are some tips.

Consider both sides of the argument. Then think about the person you're trying to persuade— what might be some objections? Have counterarguments ready.

Think of some examples to support your side—do your homework by researching the topic or talking to people who can be experts for you.

Outline your argument ahead of time. When you're ready, explain your reasoning, speak calmly, and listen! Practice some persuasive writing on these pages.

_____

_____

_____

_____

_____

_____

_____

_____

_____

_____

_____

_____

_____

_____

_____

_____

_____

_____

_____

_____

_____

_____

_____

_____

_____

Fitting In Is Out

welcome to
Monster High!

CLEO DE NILE

RAD Intel Party

NICKNAME: Your Highness

CATCHPHRASES: Golden! Royal!

FAVORITE CLASS: Geometry, because anything that involves triangles and pyramids is as easy as π

LEAST FAVORITE CLASS: History—been there, seen that, already has autographs from all the major players

PETS: A snake named Hissette, seven cats, various house birds

MUST-WEAR ACCESSORY: Hissette worn as an armband... and, of course, a crown!

FAVE COLOR: Gold

BEDROOM SITCH: A landscape complete with sandy island, lotus reeds, river, and skylight

BONUS TRIVIA

Can you name all of Cleo's cats?

Deuce's Wild

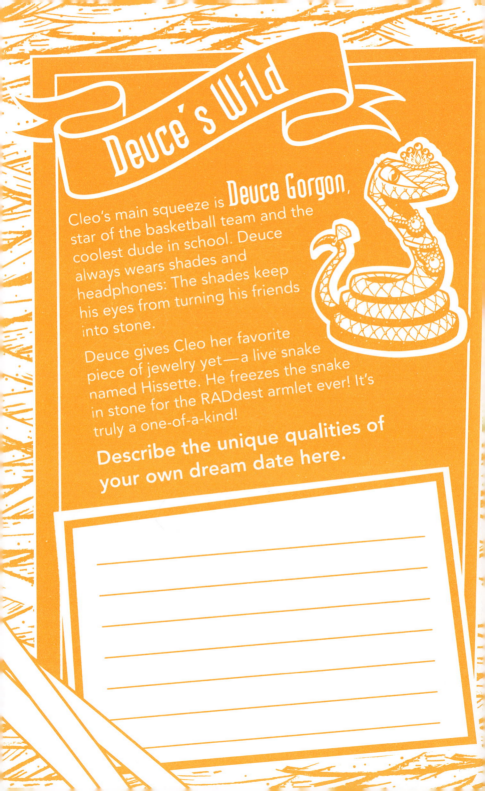

Cleo's main squeeze is **Deuce Gorgon**, star of the basketball team and the coolest dude in school. Deuce always wears shades and headphones: The shades keep his eyes from turning his friends into stone.

Deuce gives Cleo her favorite piece of jewelry yet—a live snake named Hissette. He freezes the snake in stone for the RADdest armlet ever! It's truly a one-of-a-kind!

Describe the unique qualities of your own dream date here.

_____

_____

_____

_____

_____

_____

MUMMY MOGUL

Cleo wants to have her own line of **pharaoh-fabulous jewelry**. If you were to start your own company, what would you call it?

What would your logo look like? Sketch some ideas here.

JEWEL
of the NILE

Help Cleo launch her line by designing some jewelry. Start with earrings, a bracelet, and a necklace. Top it off with some serious sparkle — a huge ring!

EARRINGS

BRACELET

NECKLACE

HUGE RING!

FREAK C'EST CHIC FASHION

Cleo is always at the height of fashion and up on the latest trends, but she also likes to add an Egyptian twist—some gold jewelry, snake bangles, or jeweled headbands. Look through your closet and plan some outfits for days when you want to look as if you just stepped out of *Teen Vogue*! Sketch the outfits on these pages for easy reference.

FREAK
C'EST
CHIC
FASHION

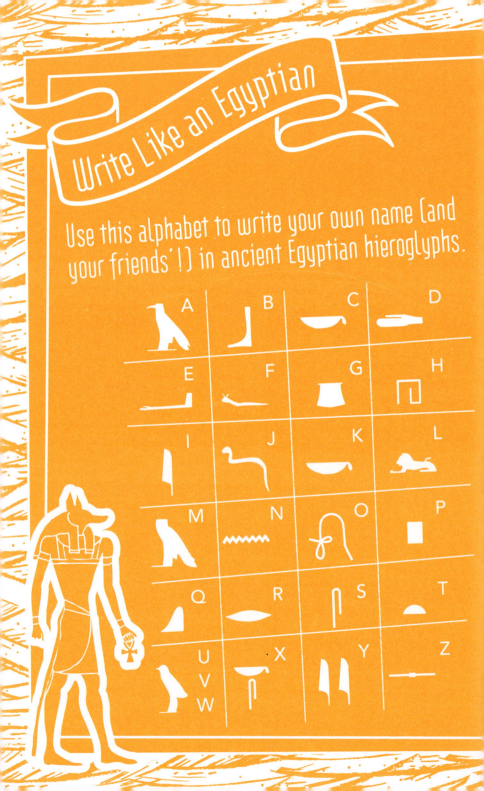

Write Like an Egyptian

Use this alphabet to write your own name (and your friends'!) in ancient Egyptian hieroglyphs.

A	B	C	D
E	F	G	H
I	J	K	L
M	N	O	P
Q	R	S	T
U V W	X	Y	Z

ROYAL BEAUTY

Cleo maintains a strict beauty regimen. Steal these royal secrets to keep your skin looking great.

Golden Glow

Nothing says Cairo couture like a flawless face. **Everyone in the de Nile family uses honey for preservation.** Make this honey mask at home!

You will need:
1 tablespoon honey
1 egg yolk
1/2 teaspoon almond oil
1 tablespoon yogurt

Mix all ingredients in a bowl until thick and creamy. Apply the mixture to your face, wait five minutes, and then wash it off!

Scent of a Queen

Inner beauty counts just as much as outer beauty. **Nothing calms Cleo's royal nerves like lavender.** Lavender oil in a bath, lavender-scented candles, and a little lavender perfume can calm the crazy world around you.

Pharaoh Snacks

Her Highness snacks on grapes — and not just because they won't smear her lip gloss. Grape skins are full of antioxidants, nature's antiaging miracle.

_____ **Omigeb!**

Mummy Knows Best!

Golden!

Royal!

CLAWDEEN WOLF

RAD Intel Party

NICKNAME: Deenie

CATCHPHRASE: Fur real!

FAVORITE CLASS: Economics, so she can work on building her own DIY business empire

LEAST FAVORITE CLASS: Astronomy—she doesn't need to know any more about the moon!

PETS: The house is full of wolves already!

MUST-HAVE ACCESSORY: Custom-painted nails

FAVE COLOR: Purple (especially with gold!)

BEDROOM SITCH: A pad filled with DIY flair—spray-painted fencing as a headboard, crushed-glass mosaics, and lots and lots of shoe racks!

BONUS TRIVIA
Can you name all of Clawdeen's siblings?

MONSTER HIGH ™

IT'S MY PAR-TAY

Start planning now to have a birthday part-ay
as freaky-fabulous as Clawdeen's Sassy Sixteen!

Potential Locations

Potential Themes

Food and Drink

Decorations

Playlist

Where There's a Wolf, There's a Way

clawdeenwolf | 28 videos ▼ | | subscribe | 4,255,890 views

▶ ◀ ↗

Clawdeen starts a video blog to share her do-it-yourself tips for fashion and decorating. Try it yourself! Make a video blog alone or with a friend. Not sure what to do? Here are some suggestions.

- 🐾 Read a poem.
- 🐾 Perform a monologue from a play.
- 🐾 Talk about something in the news, and give your opinion.
- 🐾 Talk about your favorite TV show or movie.
- 🐾 Review a book.
- 🐾 Cook a recipe step-by-step.
- 🐾 Share your own DIY tips.

Your Ideas

FREAK C'EST CHIC FASHION

Clawdeen loves to make her own clothes. She's inspired by street fashion and high fashion at the same time—she can easily switch back and forth between sporty and glam. She might mix a cropped hoodie with a glitter top and skinny jeans. She also loves a touch of fur, natch—and if you can't grow your own, go faux! Look through your closet and plan some outfits for days when you want to look street cool with a fashion-forward edge! Sketch the outfits on these pages for easy reference.

FREAK
C'EST
CHIC
FASHION

Clawdeen RAD DIY

If Clawdeen accidentally claws one of her shirts, she turns it into fashion! Get your own clawed look — it's perfect for layering, and it's a cinch to make!

1 Take a slightly baggy T-shirt and fold it in half lengthwise (down the middle).

2 Use scissors to cut horizontal slits across the shirt starting at the fold. Snip the slits about a half inch apart, leaving three to four inches at the bottom of the shirt unsnipped.

3 Unfold, stretch the tee to make the strips curl, and rock the shredded look!

0 1 2 3 4 5 6 7 8 9 10

TOTALLY SHREDDED TEE

MOSAIC MIRROR FRAME

Honor your friends by framing a photo of them. This mosaic is made of mirror pieces, so anytime you look at it, you'll see yourself in the picture too!

You will need:

- 🐾 A plain picture frame (any size and color) as a base
- 🐾 Craft or wood glue (also known as PVA glue)
- 🐾 Small reflective tiles (available at a craft store)

1 Remove the picture glass from the frame so it doesn't get scratched or become smeared with glue.

2 In a well-ventilated area, use glue to attach the reflective tiles to your frame, one at a time until the frame is covered. It's up to you how much space to leave between each piece!

Let the glue dry thoroughly before putting the frame back together and adding a fave photo! **3**

Who Let the Wolf Out?

At her Sassy Sixteen birthday party, Clawdeen finally relaxes enough to just be herself. Can you think of a time when you were comfortable enough to let others see the real you? Whom were you with? Can you be yourself all the time? Why or why not?

FUR IS THE NEW BLACK!

FUR REAL!

DRACULAURA

RAD Intel Party

NICKNAMES: Lala, Ula D

CATCHPHRASE: Fangtastic!

FAVORITE CLASS: Creative writing, because she loves to write about all her friends!

LEAST FAVORITE CLASS: Geography—after 1,599 years, she's been everywhere...twice!

PETS: A few bats in the belfry

MUST-CARRY ACCESSORY: Parasol, to keep the sun off her skin!

FAVE COLOR: Pink

BEDROOM SITCH: A sumptuous confection of lace and tulle draped around a velvet-lined coffin— designed by Uncle Vlad, of course

BONUS TRIVIA

What kind of car does Lala drive?

JET SET

Lala has been alive for almost sixteen hundred years, and she's traveled the world. What places do you want to visit?

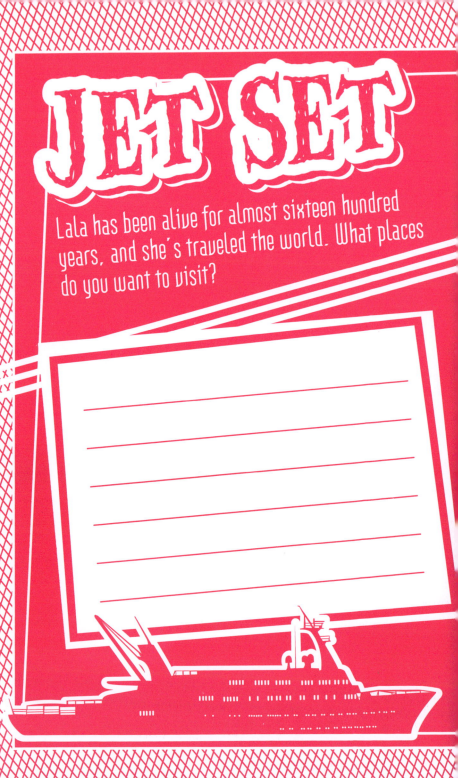

FREAK C'EST CHIC FASHION

Lala's always cold, so she turns heads by turning up the heat with layers and lots of stylish knits. Even a minidress can work in cold weather if you add tights, a vest, and arm warmers on top. Look through your closet and plan some outfits for chilly days when you crave sizzling chic! Sketch the outfits on these pages for easy reference.

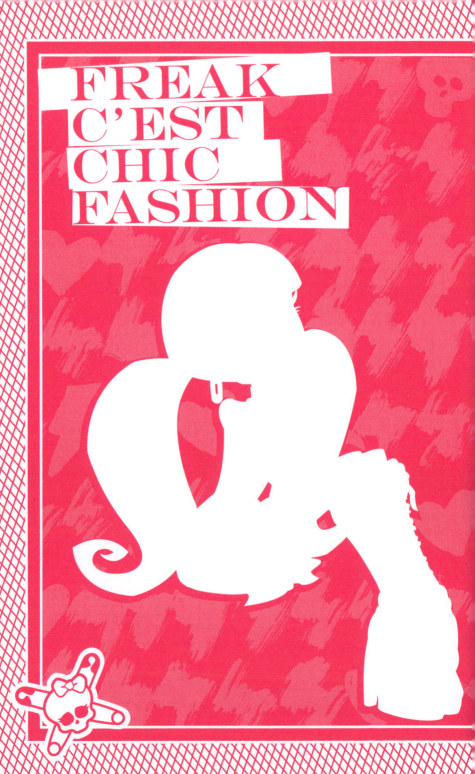

Vegetarian Vamp

Unlike most vampires, Draculaura can't stand the sight or taste of blood! She's on a strictly vegetarian diet, and she's smart enough to make sure she gets plenty of vitamins and minerals:

Iron Dried beans and fruits are good sources of iron.

Vitamin B-12 Look for foods fortified with B-12, or take a daily multivitamin.

Vitamin D You may need a supplement if, like Lala, you don't get much sun.

Calcium Spinach, kale, and broccoli are good sources of calcium.

Zinc Toss back some nuts for a snack that packs zinc.

Consult a nutritionist or your doctor to make sure your vegetarian diet is healthful and balanced!

LALA BEAUTY TIP

Never leave home without a daily sunscreen—at least 15 SPF. If you're going to spend time in the sun, apply two tablespoons of sunscreen all over at least a half hour before heading outdoors. Remember to reapply every two hours!

Love Bites

Need a sweet treat to bring to a party or give to a valentine? Whip up these vegan cupcakes with Lala's recipe. **They're red velvet, of course!**

Note from Lala: Have an adult around to help mix these up— and to keep an eye on the oven!

The recipe makes about two dozen cupcakes.

You will need:

For the cake
2 cups soy milk
2 teaspoons apple cider vinegar
2-1/2 cups all-purpose flour
4 tablespoons cocoa powder
1 teaspoon baking powder
1 teaspoon baking soda
1 teaspoon salt
2/3 cup coconut oil
2 ounces red food coloring
4 teaspoons vanilla extract
1-1/2 cups agave nectar (or
   2 cups granulated sugar)
24 cupcake liners

For the frosting
1/4 cup softened margarine
1/4 cup softened dairy-free
   cream cheese substitute
1 teaspoon vanilla extract
2 cups confectioners sugar

1 **Preheat the oven** to 350 degrees.

2 In a medium bowl, **add the apple cider vinegar to the soy milk**. Set the liquid mixture aside.

3 In a large bowl, **combine all the dry ingredients**: flour, cocoa powder, baking powder, baking soda, and salt.

4 **Stir coconut oil, food coloring, and vanilla extract** into the liquid mixture.

5 Slowly **pour the liquid mixture and the agave nectar** into the dry ingredients. Mix until well blended.

6 **Fill cupcake liners** with batter until each is three-quarters full.

7 **Bake about 20 minutes** – until you can poke the cake with a toothpick and it comes out clean. Place the cupcakes on a rack to cool.

8 To **make the frosting**, beat together the margarine, dairy-free cream cheese, and vanilla extract until creamy.

9 Slowly **add the confectioners sugar** and beat until smooth.

10 **Frost the cupcakes** after they have cooled completely!

MIRROR IMAGE

MIRROR IMAGE

Clawd helps Lala conquer her most annoying vamp side effect: She can't see herself in the mirror! Being able to apply lip gloss anytime is a valuable skill for a girl to have! Practice putting on lipstick freehand.

1 Open your mouth.

2 Are you a lefty or a righty? Use the hand you write with to hold the lipstick. Starting at the center of your upper lip, draw half a heart on each side. Repeat on your lower lip.

3 Use your fingertip to trace around the outside of your lips to remove any stray gloss or lipstick.

4 Check the mirror to see how fangtastic you look!

BONUS IDEA

Take your skills to the next level: Practice whipping up a cool new updo without a mirror. Then you'll be ready to go after a workout, gym class, or a trip to the beach!

BFF VERSUS BF?

Lala is in a tough spot when she has to choose between Clawdeen and Clawd. Has a friend ever wanted you to choose her over your man (or vice versa)? What did you do? Can you think of any situations in which you might do the opposite?

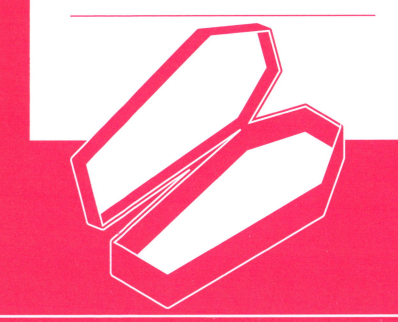

SWEET 1600!

LAGOONA BLUE

RAD Intel Party

NICKNAME: Blue

CATCHPHRASES: Ace! Bonzer!

FAVORITE CLASS: Oceanography— if she can't be in the water, she wants to be studying it!

LEAST FAVORITE CLASS: Biology, because she protests against the lab requirement. Save the frogs!

PETS: Never met a fish she didn't want to take home

MUST-HAVE ACCESSORIES: Elbow-length gloves and lots of moisturizer!

FAVE COLOR: Ocean blue

BEDROOM SITCH: At her aunt and uncle's house in America, she misses easy access to the beach—but an in-room water tank makes Blue feel right at home!

BONUS TRIVIA

Name Blue's aunt whom she stays with in Salem.

_____

What's the name of the beach Blue calls home?

_____

Water Power

Coming from Australia and being a sea monster, Blue wants to save sea creatures and protect Earth's oceans and marine environments—especially her home continent's coral reefs. Want to help? For starters, check out these organizations, and then look for more information on your own. You could even start your own club at school!

Save My Oceans
www.savemyoceans.com

The Nature Conservancy: Oceans and Coasts
www.nature.org/initiatives/marine

Coral Reef Alliance
www.coral.org

Save the Whales
www.savethewhales.org

WHAT I WANT TO DO TO HELP:

_____

_____

_____

_____

_____

_____

_____

_____

_____

Say What, Sheila?

Sometimes it's hard to figure out what Blue is saying! Use this **glossary** to suss out her lingo from Down Under!

ace
excellent!

bizzo
business—as in, anyone trying to read your diary better mind his own bizzo!!

bludger
a lazy person or a killjoy

bodgy
inferior, of poor quality

bogged
stuck in the mud

bonzer
great!

boomer
the boss, the man in charge... but literally, a big male kangaroo

fair dinkum
true, real—as in, I'm a fair dinkum RAD!

g'day
typical Down Under greeting

gobsmacked
totally surprised

lippy
lip balm

mad as a cut snake
really, really mad

mates
friends

rack off
get lost!

ripper
awesome!

sheila
any girl, especially if you don't know her name

shonky
doubtful, suspect, dubious

sparklers
jewels, such as Cleo's ace gems

spewin'
really angry

FREAK C'EST CHIC FASHION

Blue does dress up sometimes, but she usually flaunts a sporty look between swim practices—she's always ready to hit the water! Look through your closet and plan some swimsuit cover-ups to make a splash as you head from beach to boutique! Sketch the outfits on these pages for easy reference.

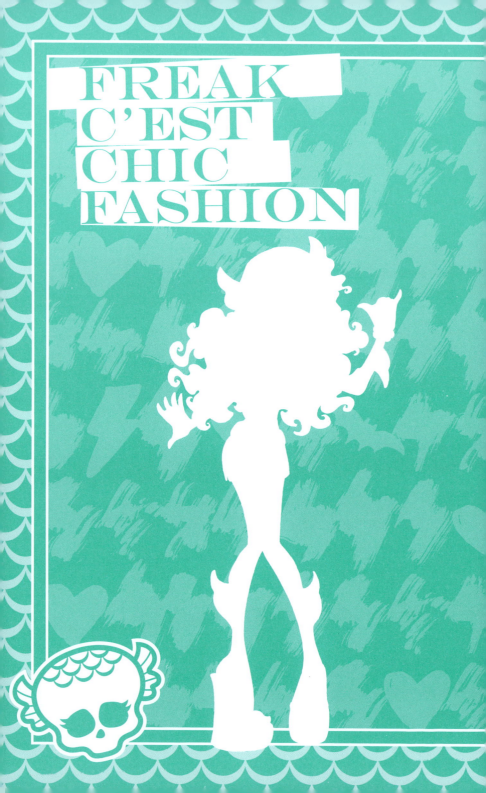

FREAK
C'EST
CHIC
FASHION

BONZER BRACELET

Lagoona Blue and Clawdeen make these awesome safety-pin bracelets. Create your own bauble — it's a sea breeze!

You will need:

50 to 70 large safety pins
(silver, gold, or your favorite color)

Beads in your best colors
(about 15 per pin)

Two 10-inch lengths of
elastic cord

1 Open the safety pins and thread them with beads. Watch out for the sharp points! Close the beaded pins.

2 Thread one elastic cord through the hole at the bottom of one beaded pin. Next, thread the same cord through the closed end of a second pin. Continue adding pins, alternating holes as you thread the cord.

3 Thread the second cord through the opposite end of the pins.

4 There should be excess elastic at the end of each cord. Gently fit the bracelet around your wrist to check the size. Then tie the opposite ends of each cord to fit. Make the bracelet snug against your wrist. Since the bands are stretchy, you'll still be able to slide your ripper bracelet on and off easily!

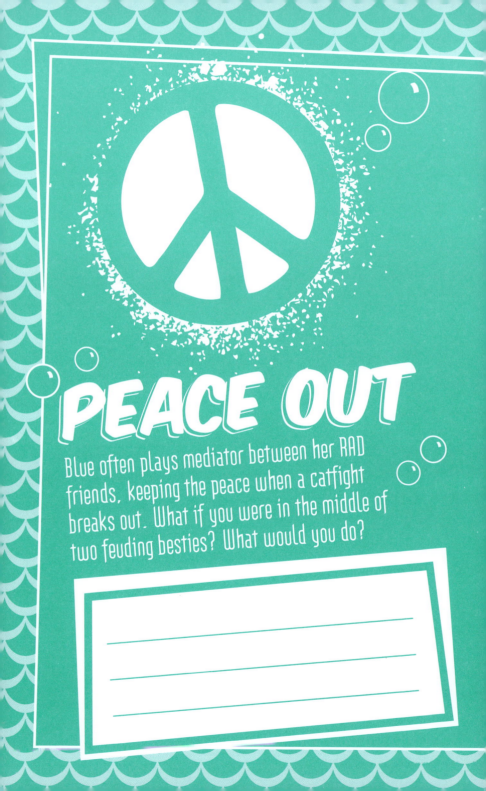

PEACE OUT

Blue often plays mediator between her RAD friends, keeping the peace when a catfight breaks out. What if you were in the middle of two feuding besties? What would you do?

ACE!

_____

_____

_____

_____

_____

_____

_____

_____

_____

_____

_____

BONZER!

Answer Skeleton Key

POWER PUZZLE

Are you all powered up? Check the grid to make sure you CHARGEd it correctly.

H	R	A	C	G	E
C	E	G	A	H	R
R	C	H	E	A	G
A	G	E	H	R	C
E	A	R	G	C	H
G	H	C	R	E	A

Monster Love

Love is a battlefield—did you guess the right boy for each heart on the graph? Check the answers below!

Can Frankie see him as more than a friend?
Billy

Sparks fly with this flirtation.
D.J.

He's Romeo to her Juliet.
Brett

BONUS TRIVIA

Hey, ghouls! Are you mortalfied that you couldn't answer all the Bonus Trivia questions? Don't sweat it. Show your ghoul spirit by looking up the answers in the Monster High books by Lisi Harrison. Here are some hints....

FRANKIE STEIN BONUS TRIVIA:
Can you name all of the Glitterati?
The answer can be found on page 31 of Monster High 2: The Ghoul Next Door.

MELODY CARVER BONUS TRIVIA:
What is the name of Melody's birth mom?
The answer can be found on page 238 of Monster High 3: Where There's a Wolf, There's a Way.

CLEO DE NILE BONUS TRIVIA:
Can you name all of Cleo's cats?
The answer can be found on page 43 of Monster High 2: The Ghoul Next Door.

CLAWDEEN WOLF BONUS TRIVIA:
Can you name all of Clawdeen's siblings?
The answer can be found on pages 2–6 of Monster High 3: Where There's a Wolf, There's a Way.

DRACULAURA BONUS TRIVIA:
What kind of car does Lala drive?
The answer can be found on page 81 of Monster High.

LAGOONA BLUE BONUS TRIVIA:
Name Blue's aunt whom she stays with in Salem. What's the name of the beach Blue calls home?
The answers can be found on pages 20 and 21 of Monster High 3: Where There's a Wolf, There's a Way.

MONSTER HIGH

MONSTER HIGH

MONSTER HIGH 3

WHERE
THERE'S
A WOLF,
THERE'S
A WAY

BY THE #1 BESTSELLING AUTHOR OF THE CLIQUE

LISI HARRISON

THE
GHOUL
NEXT
DOOR

MONSTER HIGH 4

BACK AND
DEADER
THAN EVER

THE NEW YORK TIMES BESTSELLING SERIES BY
LISI HARRISON
AUTHOR OF THE CLIQUE